What A Day!

Written by
Matthew C. Sample

Illustrated by
Riley C. Sample

AuthorHouse™
1663 Liberty Drive
Bloomington, IN 47403
www.authorhouse.com
Phone: 833-262-8899

Because of the dynamic nature of the Internet, any web addresses or links contained in this book may have changed
since publication and may no longer be valid. The views expressed in this work are solely those of the author and do not
necessarily reflect the views of the publisher, and the publisher hereby disclaims any responsibility for them.

Any people depicted in stock imagery provided by Getty Images are models,
and such images are being used for illustrative purposes only.
Certain stock imagery © Getty Images.

This book is printed on acid-free paper.

ISBN: 978-1-4389-9853-4 (sc)

Print information available on the last page.

Published by AuthorHouse 06/22/2024

authorHOUSE®

Dedicated to my son.

What a Day we will have my daddy and I.

We are going exploring way up in the sky.

What will we see who really knows.

I'll put on my socks to keep the warm in my toes.

I'll put on my coat to block all the cold.

I'll get all dressed up cap and all.

Me and my Dad are going to have a Ball.

We are going to the mountains way up high,

during the summer all the way to the sky.

There is no Snow right now so it is Great!

Got to watch the time so we don't stay to late.

What will we find, I do not know,

maybe a dinosaur wild and free,

maybe he will even be hidden in a tree?

We will play until dark

and all tired out.

When I leave he'll shout,

"come back soon!"

Then he will look up and

Gaze at the Moon.

Maybe I can take my skate boards and roll around the rocks.

I bet it would be bumpy and my head would get lots of knots.

Maybe I will wait tell we're home and wear my helmet instead.

That would be a lot better I think,

or at least that is what my Mom said.

Maybe we will climb so high in the skies,

the moon will be so close it will glow bright in my eyes.

I will take the shuttle and ride it around

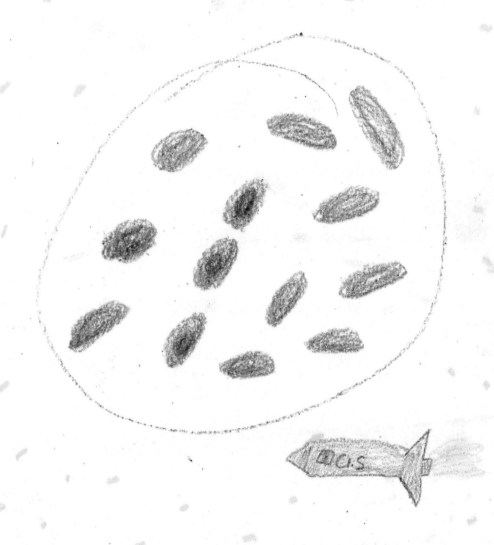

until I finally land on the ground.

The surprises I will see as around it we fly,

I will draw pictures or at least I will try.

Maybe a sea, as big as a tree,

where I can swim with the fish and they can talk to me.

There will be all sizes both great and small

and I will swim with them one and all.

With a octopus hidden in the weeds below

playing hide a seek will be the most fun of all.

I hope there is a bird that floats on the clouds.

And sings like a Queen as she whistles out loud.

Her colors all glow with the sun from behind.

I can't wait to see her as I do in my mind.

Flying so high above the trees whistling a tune

that can be heard to the far and wide.

Finally I'll come home and tell all that I found

all with excitement as I jump from the ground.

Me and my dad on this perfect day

there is nothing better that is all I will say.

Until the next time were it will be daddy and me

I will keep the excitement wondering what we will see.

Written By

Matthew C. Sample (Dad)

Pictures By

5 Year old Riley C. Sample (Me)

Edited By

Deidra A. Combs (English teacher)